First published in the United States, Great Britain, Canada, Australia, and New Zealand in 2012
by North-South Books, Inc., an imprint of NordSüd Verlag AG, CH-8005 Zürich, Switzerland.

Designed by Christy Hale.
Distributed in the United States by North-South Books Inc., New York 10016.
Library of Congress Cataloging-in-Publication Data is available.
ISBN: 978-0-7358-4087-4 (trade edition).
1 3 5 7 9 • 10 8 6 4 2
Printed in Germany by Grafisches Centrum Cuno GmbH & Co. KG, 39240 Calbe, April 2012.
www.northsouth.com

FSC
www.fsc.org
MIX
Paper from
responsible sources
FSC® C043106

SLEEPING BEAUTY

The Brothers Grimm • illustrated by Maja Dusíková

NorthSouth

New York / London

Once upon a time, a king and a queen used to say to each other every day, "If only we could have a child!" But the years came and went, and there were no children. Then one day when the queen was bathing in the lake, a frog jumped out of the water and said to her, "Your wish will be granted; and before a year has passed, you will bring a daughter into the world."

The frog's promise came true, and the queen gave birth to a daughter who was so beautiful that the king was overjoyed and decided to hold a big party. He invited not only his relatives, friends, and acquaintances, but also the fairies who lived in the land, so that they would be kind to the child. There were thirteen fairies in the kingdom, but because he only had twelve gold dishes from which they could eat, he had to leave one of the fairies out.

The party was magnificent; and when it was over, the fairies each gave the child a wonderful gift: one gave her virtue, one beauty, one wealth, and so on, until she had all that a person could wish for in this world.

When the eleventh had just finished making her presentation, the thirteenth fairy suddenly burst into the room. She wanted revenge because she hadn't been invited to the party; and without even looking at anyone or saying hello, she shouted in a very loud voice:

"When she is fifteen, the princess will be pricked by a spindle and will fall down dead!"

Without saying another word, she turned around and left the room. Everyone was shocked, but then the twelfth fairy stepped forward, because she still hadn't given the child her gift. She was not able to lift the curse of the thirteenth fairy; but she did have the power to soften it, and so she said:

"The princess will not fall down dead, but she will sleep for a hundred years."

The king, who was desperate to protect his beloved daughter from this disaster, gave orders that every spindle in the kingdom should be burned.

The promises given by the other fairies all came true, because the girl was so beautiful, gentle, friendly, and kind that everyone who met her could not help but love her.

It came to pass that on the very day when she turned fifteen, the king and queen had gone out and the girl was all alone in the palace. She wandered around, looking into every nook and cranny, until at last she came to an old tower.

She climbed up a narrow spiral staircase and arrived at a little door. In the lock was a rusty key; and when she turned it, the door flew open. Sitting in the tiny room was an old lady who was busily spinning her thread.

"Hello, grandmother," said the princess. "What are you doing?"

"I'm spinning," said the old lady, nodding her head.

"What is that funny thing that's jumping around?" asked the girl, grasping the spindle since she also wanted to spin. But hardly had she touched it when she pricked herself in the finger, and at once the curse was fulfilled. As soon as she felt the sting, she fell down on the bed that was in the room and lay in a deep slumber.

The slumber spread all through the palace. The king and queen, who had just come home and had entered the great hall, fell fast asleep, as did the whole court.

The horses in the stables, the doves on the roof, and the flies on the wall fell asleep as well. The fire stopped flaming, the roast

stopped sizzling, the maid stopped plucking the chicken, and the cook—who was about to tweak the kitchen boy's ear for making a mistake— let go of him and started snoring.

The wind died down, and not a leaf stirred on the trees outside the palace.

All around the palace a thorny hedge began to grow, and it grew higher and higher until finally it surrounded and covered the whole building so that nothing could be seen—not even the flag flying on top of the roof.

The story spread through the land about the beautiful sleeping princess, and they called her Sleeping Beauty. From time to time princes would come and try to force their way through the hedge and into the palace. But they could never do it, because the thorns held fast together as if they had hands; and the young men hung there, unable to escape and eventually dying a terrible death.

After many, many years another prince came to the country and heard an old man telling the tale of the thorny hedge behind which there was said to be a palace. In the palace was a beautiful princess named Sleeping Beauty, who had been asleep for a hundred years. And the king and queen and all the court were believed to be sleeping there too.

The old man's grandfather had told him that many princes had come and had tried to break through the thorny hedge, but they had hung there and had come to very sad ends. Then the young prince said, "I am not afraid. I shall go there and see the lovely Sleeping Beauty for myself."

The kind old man tried to stop him from going, but the prince wouldn't listen. However, by now the hundred years had passed, and the day had come when the princess was due to wake up.

When the prince reached the thorny hedge, it was full of large and beautiful flowers and opened all by itself and allowed him to pass through uninjured. But then the hedge closed up again behind him. In the courtyard he saw horses and hunting dogs lying fast asleep, and doves with their heads tucked under their wings.

When he entered the palace, the cook was still in the kitchen, her hand raised as if to tweak the boy's ear; and the kitchen maid was sitting in front of the chicken she was supposed to be plucking.

He went on, and in the great hall came upon all the courtiers, who were also fast asleep, as were the king and queen in their lofty thrones.

Once more he moved on, and everything was so still and silent that he could hear his own breath. At last he came to the old tower, and at the top of the steps he opened the door to the little room in which Sleeping Beauty was asleep on the bed.

She lay there and was so beautiful that he couldn't take his eyes off her. He bent down and gave her a kiss.

At the moment when his lips touched her, Sleeping Beauty opened her eyes, woke up, and smiled at him.

Then they went down the steps together and into the great hall, where the
king and queen and courtiers all woke up and gazed at one another wide-eyed.
The horses in the courtyard stood up and shook themselves; the hunting
dogs leaped to their feet and wagged their tails; the doves took their heads out

from under their wings and flew into the fields; the flies started crawling over the walls; the fire in the kitchen lit up again, flamed, flickered, and cooked the food; the roast began to sizzle; the cook tweaked the boy's ear; the boy yelled ouch; and the maid plucked the chicken.

The prince and princess had the most royal of royal weddings,
and from that day onward they lived happily ever after.

DEC   2012